DiSNEP · PIXAR

Cars

Adapted by Ben Smiley
Illustrated by Jean-Paul Orpiñas and Scott Tilley
Designed by Winnie Ho

Inspired by the art and character designs created by Pixar Animation Studios

🏆 A Golden Book · New York

Published in the United States by Golden Books, an imprint of Random House Children's Books, a division of Random House, Inc., New York, and in Canada by Random House of Canada Limited, Toronto, in conjunction with Disney Enterprises, Inc. Golden Books, A Golden Book, A Little Golden Book, the G colophon, and the distinctive gold spine are registered trademarks of Random House, Inc.
Library of Congress Control Number: 2005933182
ISBN-13: 978-0-7364-2347-2
ISBN-10: 0-7364-2347-8
www.goldenbooks.com
www.randomhouse.com/kids/disney
Printed in the United States of America

25 24 23 22 21 20 19 18 17 16 15 14

P9-CEN-956

Lightning McQueen was a race car! He was *flashy* red and had a SHINY lightning bolt on his side.

He even had adoring fans.

But he also had a **BiG** problem. His pit crews kept quitting. You see, McQueen thought he could do everything by himself.

And since all McQueen cared about was winning races, he didn't have any friends . . .

except **Mack**.

Mack the truck drove McQueen to all his races.

One night, McQueen wanted to get to a **really BiG** race really fast. He made Mack drive too long, and the loyal truck got **tired**.

Mack swerved, and McQueen fell out the back of the truck! **Uh-oh!**

McQueen had been sleeping.
But he woke up fast! The race car
was **LOST** and *scared*!

Soon he was
racing toward an
old forgotten
town called
Radiator
Springs.

The Sheriff chased McQueen. McQueen was scared, so he drove *faster*! He knocked into just about everything in the little town.

What a mess!

When the chase was over, McQueen had ruined the town's main street. He was in a heap of **trouble**.

In fact, the Sheriff had him towed to jail for all the damage he had done.

Only one car in town was friendly to McQueen—
a rusty tow truck named Mater. Mater didn't know
that McQueen was a famous car. He just wanted to
make a new **friend**.

Soon McQueen was
brought to court. He
thought he would be set
free because he was
a superstar race car.

He was right—almost. Doc, the town's judge, told McQueen to leave town and never come back. He didn't like race cars.

Then Sally, a blue sports car, arrived. She was a lawyer. McQueen thought Sally was pretty.

But Sally just wanted McQueen to fix the mess he had made.

The townsfolk agreed. They loved their town. So Sally and Doc made a deal: McQueen could leave **AFTER** he fixed the road.

Accused

But McQueen was still in a rush to get to his big race. So he worked too fast and made an even **BIGGER** mess of the messy road.

A little while later, the town watched as Mater tried to drive on the new road. But the road was simply too **BUMPY**.

Doc was angry. He challenged McQueen to a race. "If you win, you go and I fix the road," said Doc. "If I win, you do the road **MY** way."

It certainly looked as if
McQueen would win the race.
But he didn't. He crashed into a
cactus patch. Luckily, his new
friend, Mater, helped
him out.

After that, McQueen learned a few things.

He learned that the townsfolk were **proud** of their home.

He learned why Sally **loved** Radiator Springs.

And he learned that Doc had once been a ***champion*** race car.

Finally, McQueen fixed the road. Then he thanked all his new friends by getting spiffed up—Radiator Springs style!

Red the fire truck squirted **McQueen clean.**

Guido and Luigi gave him new **tires.**

Ramone gave
him a new
paint job.

And Flo gave
him a can of her
best oil.

By that night,
the townsfolk had
fixed their shops
and their **NEON** lights!
The **OLD** town looked
NEW again!

Soon it was time to go back to the racetrack. But now McQueen had Doc as his crew chief. He also had a new pit crew. And they weren't just his teammates— they were his new **best friends**.